Welcome to Japan

by Alison Auch

Content and Reading Adviser: Mary Beth Fletcher, Ed.D.
Educational Consultant/Reading Specialist
The Carroll School, Lincoln, Massachusetts

Spyglass
BOOKS

COMPASS POINT BOOKS

Minneapolis, Minnesota

Compass Point Books
3722 West 50th Street, #115
Minneapolis, MN 55410

Visit Compass Point Books on the Internet at *www.compasspointbooks.com*
or e-mail your request to *custserv@compasspointbooks.com*

Photographs ©: PhotoDisc, cover; Compass Point Books, cover (background); Dave Bartruff/Corbis, 4;
Corel, 6, 8, 9, 10, 12, 14, 15, 16, 17; Craig Lovell/Corbis, 7; Stephanie Maze/Corbis, 11;
John Dakers/Corbis, 13.

Project Manager: Rebecca Weber McEwen
Editor: Heidi Schoof
Photo Selectors: Rebecca Weber McEwen and Heidi Schoof
Designers: Jaime Martens and Les Tranby
Illustrator: Svetlana Zhurkina

Library of Congress Cataloging-in-Publication Data

Auch, Alison.
  Welcome to Japan / by Alison Auch.
     p. cm. — (Spyglass books)
Includes bibliographical references and index.
  ISBN 0-7565-0368-X
  1. Japan—Juvenile literature. I. Title.
  II. Series.
  DS806 .A86 2002
  952—dc21
                    2002002751

Contents

Where Is Japan?

Welcome to my country!
I live in Japan,
which is a group
of *islands* in Asia.
I want to tell you about
my beautiful home.

Japanese Flag

Did You Know?

Japan has four main islands
and thousands of smaller ones.

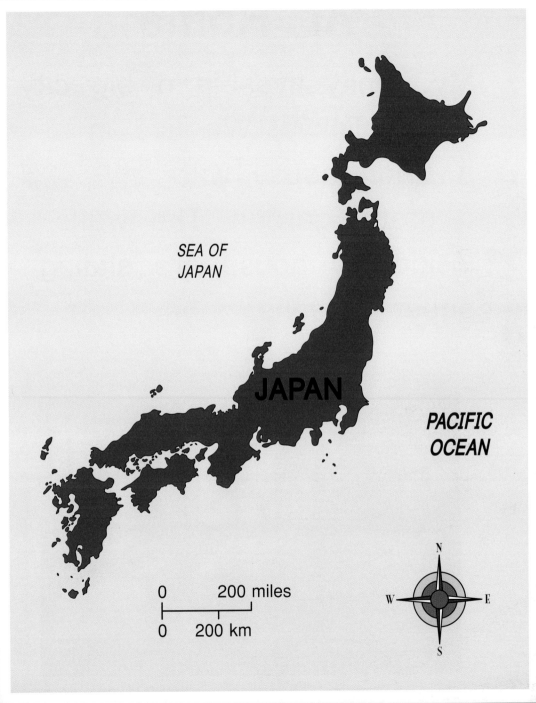

SEA OF
JAPAN

JAPAN

PACIFIC
OCEAN

0   200 miles

0   200 km

N
W   E
S

At Home

My family lives in a big city called Tokyo. We live in a small house with a pretty garden. The walls inside my house are sliding paper screens.

My grandparents live in a beautiful house in the country like this one.

At Work

My father works for
a company that makes
computers. My mother has
a shop that sells plants.
Sometimes she lets
me help her.

Most people ride the train
and then walk to work.

Something's Fishy!

In Japan, people eat rice at almost every meal. People also eat **seafood.** We often eat our fish raw. Raw fish and **vinegar** with rice is called "sushi."

Rice is the main crop that is grown in Japan.

Sushi

Clothes for All Events

Most people in Japan wear modern clothes. We wear *kimonos* during holidays and festivals. One of our main holidays is the New Year.

This girl is wearing a kimono.

The Tea Ceremony

In Japan, the tea ceremony is very important. A tea master serves tea to people in a beautiful and special way. My aunt is a tea master.

Tea ceremonies make people feel peaceful.

Fun Facts

Many people in Japan travel on fast trains called bullet trains.

Bonsai trees are tiny trees. They have been shaped to look like full-grown trees.

In Japan, most children wear uniforms to school.

Some Japanese gardens only have sand and stones.

Japan has very pretty cherry trees. People travel from all over to see the trees when they are in bloom.

The Crane Woman

Once upon a time,
a man found a hurt **crane**
in the forest. He was kind
to her, and he helped her.
When she was well,
she flew away.

A year later, the man met a beautiful woman and they were married.

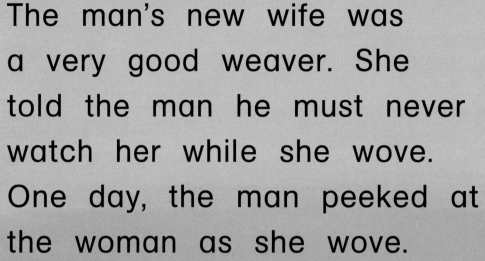

The man's new wife was a very good weaver. She told the man he must never watch her while she wove. One day, the man peeked at the woman as she wove.

She was the crane
he had saved! Because
the man had seen her,
the crane had to leave.
Sadly, she flew away.

Glossary

crane–a water bird with long legs, a long neck, and big wings

island–an area of land surrounded by water

kimono–a long robe with big sleeves worn by people in Japan

seafood–food that comes from the sea, or ocean, such as fish or lobster

vinegar–a sour liquid used for making foods, such as salad dressing

Learn More

Books

Harvey, Miles. *Look What Came From Japan.* New York: Franklin Watts, 1999.

Heinrichs, Ann. *Japan.* New York: Children's Press, 1997.

Pluckrose, Henry. *Japan.* New York: Franklin Watts, 1998.

Web Sites

www.ipl.org/youth/cquest

jin.jcic.or.jp/kidsweb/

Index

GR: G
Word Count: 250

From Alison Auch

Reading and writing are my favorite things to do. When I'm not reading or writing, I like to go to the mountains or play with my little girl, Chloe.